Peeps
BRAND

Let Your PEEPSonality Shine!

How to live
the sweet life
like a PEEP

ISBN 978-1-5247-1910-4 (trade) — ISBN 978-1-5247-1911-1 (ebook)
randomhousekids.com

Printed in the United States of America
10 9 8 7 6 5 4 3 2 1

Let Your PEEPSonality Shine!

How to live the sweet life like a PEEP

By Andrea Posner-Sanchez

Random House 🏠 **New York**

If you've noticed that your peeps don't seem that into you lately, perhaps it's time to work on your **PEEPSonality**®.

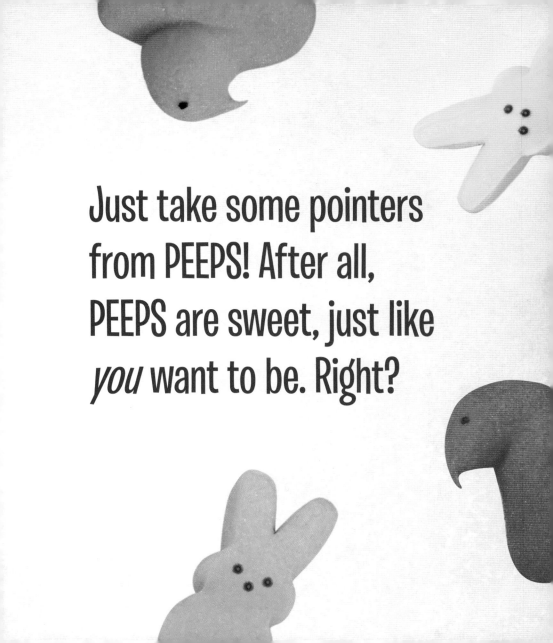

Just take some pointers from PEEPS! After all, PEEPS are sweet, just like *you* want to be. Right?

First impressions
are important.
Always remember
to

Smile!

PEEPS don't smile, but they do bring a smile to the face of everyone who eats them.

A sense of humor is key.
Be funny.

Q : What do you call
a mini PEEP?

A : A PEEPSqueak!

Don't keep your friends waiting. Try to be on time.

Work hard and be **responsible**.

PEEPS used to have their faces stamped on by hand!

But take time to stop
and smell the roses.

Laugh often—and **loud**.

Be a good listener.

Don't be too set in your ways—change can be good.

A good PEEPS change:
In 1953, it took **27 hours** to create one PEEPS® marshmallow chick by hand with a pastry tube. Today, thanks to changes in technology, it takes roughly **six minutes**.

Celebrations are always better with **chocolate!**

Chocolate-dipped and chocolate-covered PEEPS chicks were introduced in 2010.

Be kind to the Earth. Recycle!

FUN FACT

Enough PEEPS are made each
year to circle the Earth
two times!

Be a good friend.

Be accepting of others.

Remember . . .

inside, we are all the **same**!

Don't be afraid to try a new look.

PEEPS chicks used to have wings! Looking to achieve a sleeker, more modern look, the wings were "clipped" in 1955.

An employee at Just Born, the company that makes PEEPS, invented chocolate "jimmies" or sprinkles. And yes, his name was **Jimmy**.

Reach out to friends

you've lost touch with.

Due to popular demand, white PEEPS chicks came back after a ten-year hiatus.

Here are more fun facts to share with your friends:

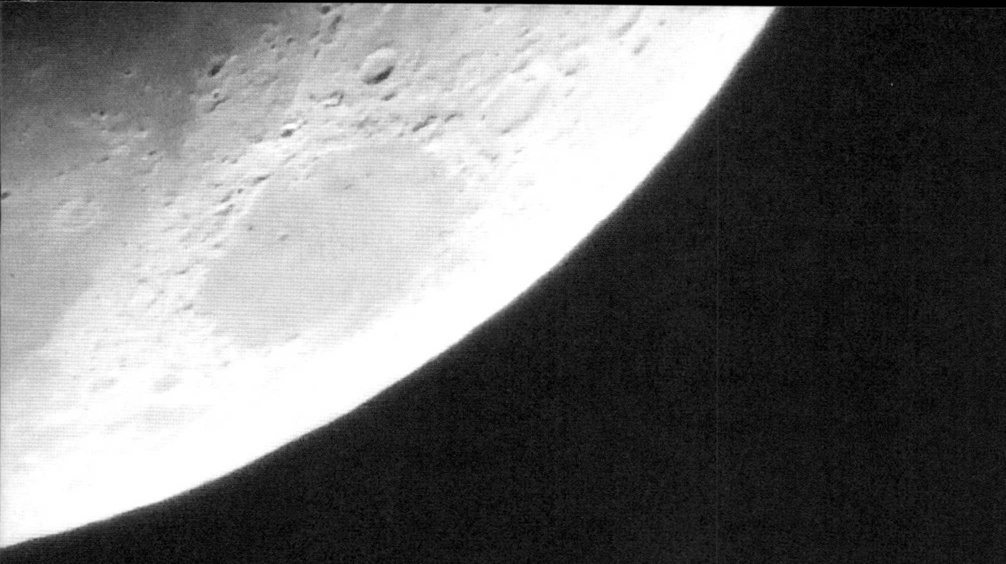

It would take
429 million PEEPS
bunnies to circle
the moon.

According to the U.S. Census Bureau, a baby is born every eight seconds.

At Just Born, 504 PEEPS are hatched every eight seconds.

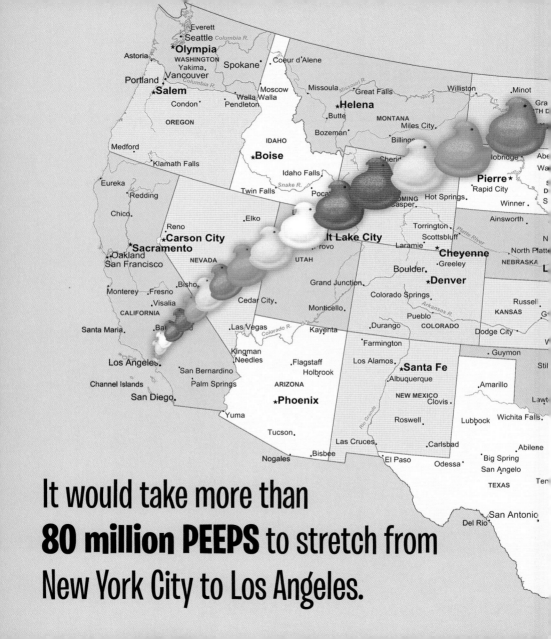

It would take more than **80 million PEEPS** to stretch from New York City to Los Angeles.

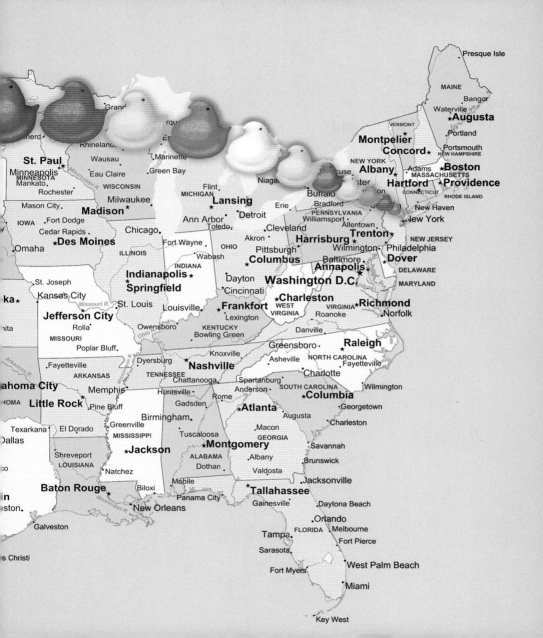

It would take roughly **110,000 PEEPS** chicks to equal the weight of the Liberty Bell.

It would take more than **3.9 million PEEPS** chicks to cover the floor of the White House.

One T. rex weighed about the same as 847,000 PEEPS.

Yellow is America's best-selling color of PEEPS, followed by **pink** and then **blue.**

It would take **127 quadrillion PEEPS** to fill the Grand Canyon.

Nearly **9,000 PEEPS** bunnies stacked on top of one another would reach the top of the Empire State Building.

It would take **17 days, 6 hours,** and **3 minutes** to make enough PEEPS to line the length of the Rocky Mountains.

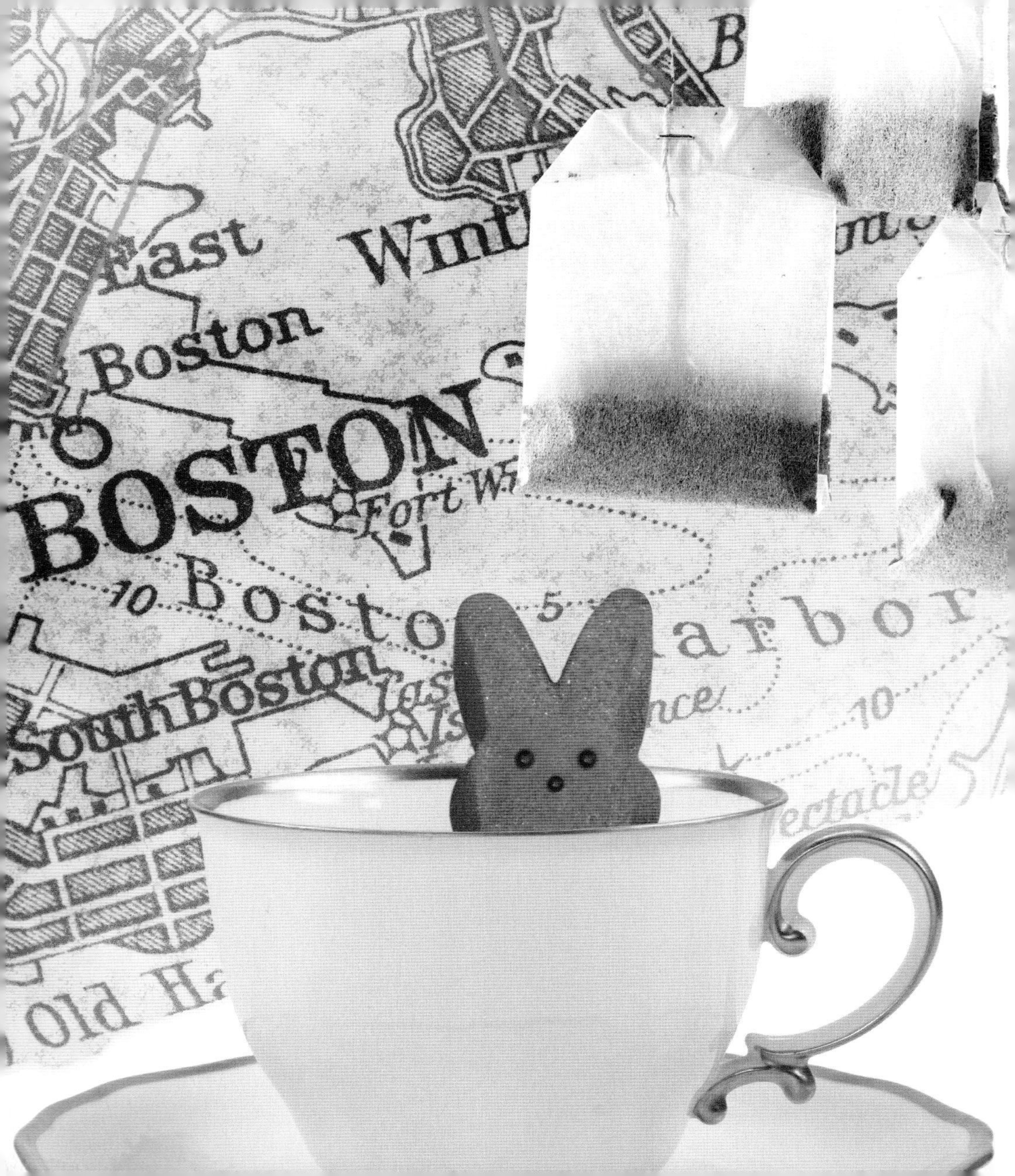
East
Boston
BOSTON
10
Bosto
5
arbor
South Boston
10
Old

More than 90,000 pounds of tea were dumped into Boston Harbor during the Boston Tea Party. That's equivalent to the weight of more than **4.7 million PEEPS**.

It would take **560,000 PEEPS** to cover the famous Hollywood sign.

KEEP
CALM
&
Peep
On